THIS BOOK BELONGS

I wrote this story for my future children,
god-children and the kids who will not be related to me
but will call me 'aunty' anyway.
So that they can have books in their mother tongues
that won't just be a translation
of a story written by certain demographics, but
one that they could genuinely
relate to.

However, I dedicate this book to all the milennial parents,
aunties, uncles and godparents of African and
Afro-Caribbean heritage who have
ever been told:
"There's rice at home."

One day, Dámi and Ṣèyí went to the market with their mummy to buy food for the house.

As they were walking home, they saw an ice cream van.

"Mummy!" Ṣèyí called, "I want to eat ice cream."

"Ṣèyí," Mummy answered, "there's rice at home."

Soon after, Dámi saw a burger van.

"Mummy, can you please give us money to buy burgers and chips?" Dámi asked.

"Do you have burger and chips money?" Mummy replied. "There's rice at home."

Not long after this, Seyi saw a man selling sweets.

"Mummy, can we have money to buy sweets please?" Seyi pleaded.

"Haven't I told you already that there is rice at home?" Mummy replied sounding a little cross.

When they arrived home, they found Daddy cooking in the kitchen.

"Hello my lovely wife and children," Daddy greeted.

"Dinner is almost ready, go and wash your hands" he said.

When Dámi and Ṣèyí
sat down for dinner,
they were excited to see
a tub of ice cream
on the dinner table.

But when they opened the container, they found stew instead of ice cream.

This made Dámi and Ṣèyí very cross but it made Mummy and Daddy laugh.

After dinner, Dámi and Ṣèyí
went to watch telly in the living room.

To their surprise, Mummy and Daddy
came in with a big bowl of puff puff
and a big tub of ice cream.

This made Dámi and Ṣèyí very happy.

The whole family watched telly together until it was time for bed.

The End.

This book is available in multiple languages
spoken across Africa & the Caribbean.
If you'd like more books
like this please, email:
hello@preciousma.co.uk